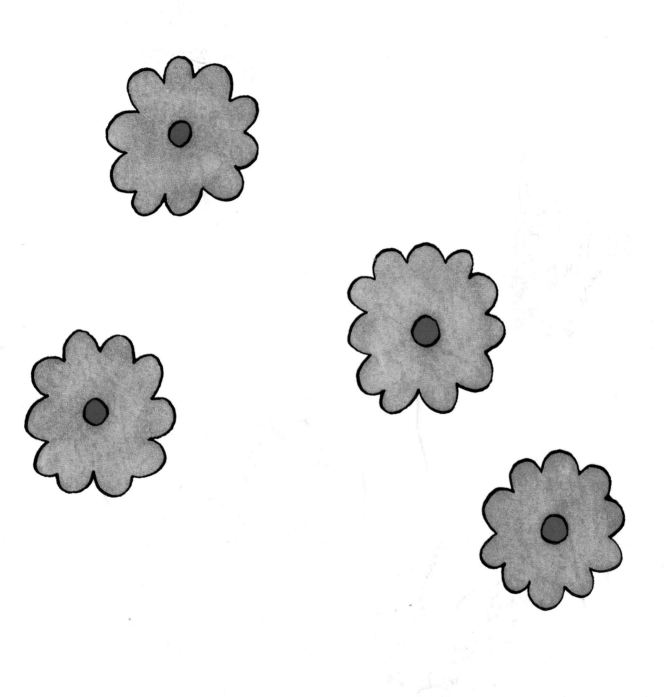

For
Caroline

First published 1992 by Walker Books Ltd
87 Vauxhall Walk, London SE11 5HJ

This edition published 2007

4 6 8 10 9 7 5 3

This book has been typeset in AT Arta.

Printed in China

British Library Cataloguing in Publication Data:
a catalogue record for this book is
available from the British Library.

ISBN 978-1-4063-0991-1

www.walkerbooks.co.uk

Smart Auntie

Nick Sharratt

WALKER BOOKS
AND SUBSIDIARIES
LONDON · BOSTON · SYDNEY · AUCKLAND

When my seven
smart aunties came for
the day, Auntie Sue
wore blue,

Auntie Dots
wore spots,

Auntie Etta
wore a sweater,

Auntie Tracey
wore something
lacy,

Auntie Molly
had a brolly,

Auntie Pat
had a
flowery hat,

and Auntie Madge
had a cap
with a badge,

because she was driving the coach.

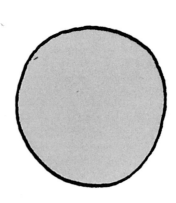